The Tale of a Naughty Little Rabbit

In a snug little burrow
beneath a tall fir tree,
in the heart of the wood,
lived a family of rabbits.

There was Mrs. Rabbit and
her three little daughters —

Flopsy

Mopsy

Cotton-tail

who were all as good as gold.

And then
there was Peter.

Here he is, LOOK!
One naughty little rabbit
wearing his new blue coat.

Today, Mrs. Rabbit had some shopping to do. "You can play outside while I'm gone," she told her children, "But remember – STAY AWAY from Mr. McGregor's garden!"

Mr. Rabbit had visited that garden once. . .

. . .and had **never** come home.

While Mrs. Rabbit was out,
Flopsy, Mopsy and Cotton-tail
busied themselves like good
little bunnies, picking wild
blackberries for supper.

But not Peter . . .

He ran straight to
Mr. McGregor's garden.

Here he is, LOOK!
One naughty little rabbit
squeezing himself under the gate.

First Peter **ate** some juicy fresh lettuces.

Then he **nibbled** some spicy red radishes.

Then he **gobbled** some crunchy green beans.

Soon, Peter's tummy began to feel a bit **funny**. He looked around for some parsley.

But instead, he found . . .

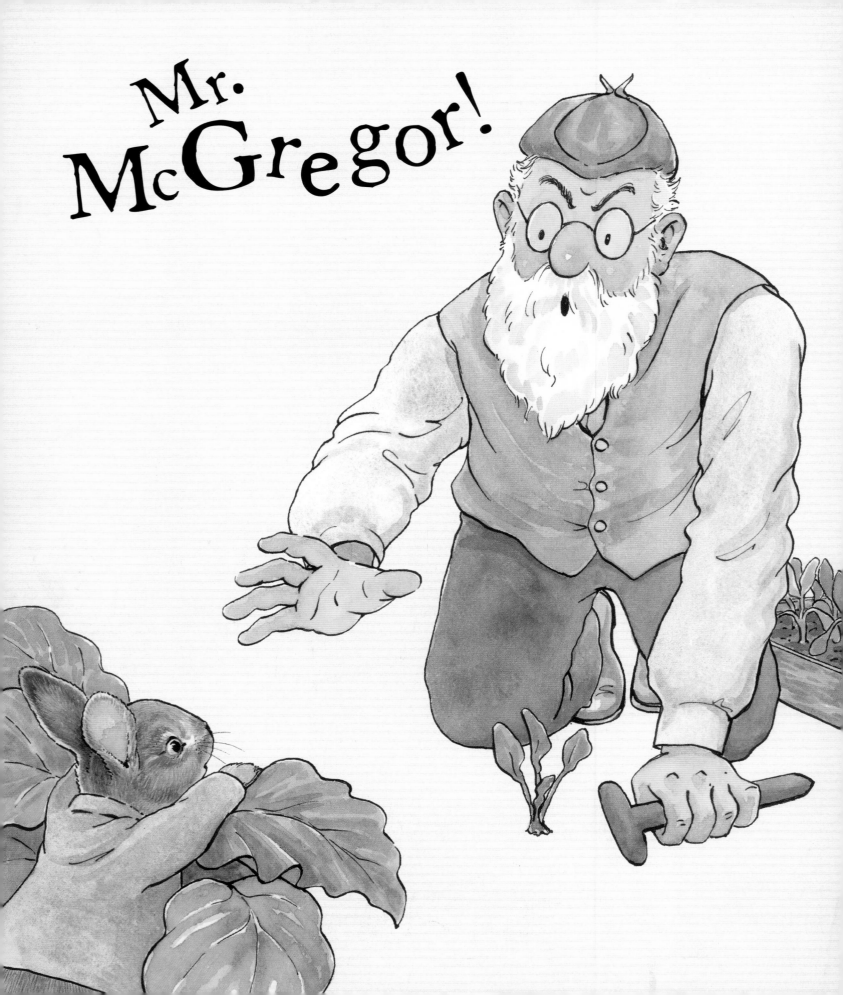

Mr.
McGregor!

Peter turned and ran as **fast** as his little rabbit legs would carry him.

But Mr. McGregor chased after him, waving a rake and shouting,

"Stop thief!"

Poor Peter was very **frightened**.
In his panic, he couldn't remember
the way back to the garden gate.

He ran back and forth, all over the garden,
with Mr. McGregor close **behind** him.

Here he is, LOOK!
One naughty little rabbit
running for his life!

As Peter **dashed** through the vegetable patch, one of his shoes fell off.

Peter kept running.

He lost his other shoe among the potato plants.

Without his shoes, Peter ran **even faster. . .**

. . . straight into the netting around the gooseberry bushes! The big brass buttons of Peter's blue coat got tangled up in the net. Suddenly Mr. McGregor appeared over him.

"You wretched little rabbit. I'll have you for my dinner!" growled Mr. McGregor.

Peter **wriggled** and **squirmed** to get **free**.

And just before Mr. McGregor
could trap him, Peter
escaped.

"Maybe I'll be SAFE in the toolshed," thought the scared little rabbit. A big green watering can seemed like the perfect hiding place – until Peter discovered **how much water** there was inside of it!

Mr. McGregor had followed him into the toolshed. He began turning over flowerpots, one at a time, searching for Peter.

All of a sudden, he heard a rabbity sneeze,

aCHOO!

from inside the watering can.

Poor Peter was out of the can in a **flash**. He ran away, as fast as his little rabbit legs would carry him.

He found his way, **at last**, back to the garden gate.

Finally, Peter was **safe** in the wood again. He ran all the way home, without stopping.

Mr. McGregor found the two shoes and the new blue coat that Peter had left behind. He made them into a scarecrow to **frighten away** the birds.

Back in the snug burrow, Mrs. Rabbit was **not at all** pleased that Peter had lost his shoes and coat.

That evening, Flopsy, Mopsy and Cotton-tail had a delicious feast of bread and milk and freshly picked blackberries.

And Peter?

Mrs. Rabbit put him **straight to bed** without any supper – only a spoonful of chamomile tea to settle his aching tummy.

Here he is, LOOK!
One naughty little rabbit
feeling rather sorry for himself.

Do you feel sorry for him too?

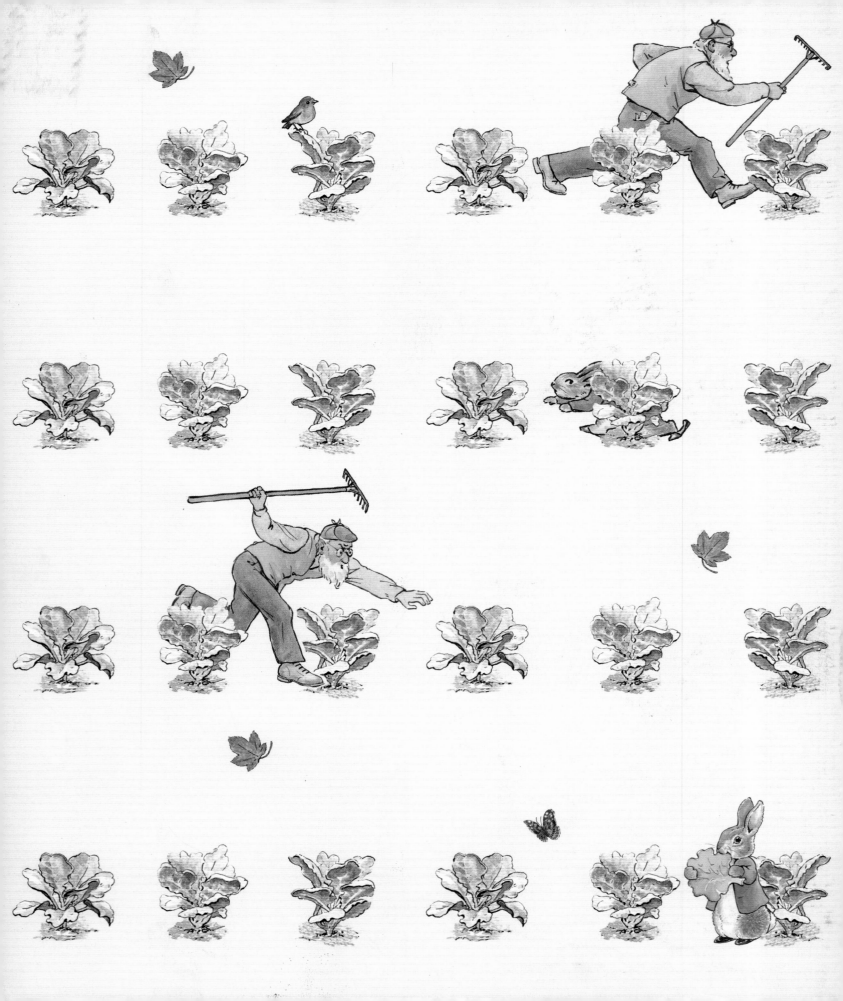